Contents

Chapter One
Scary Ladder 2

Chapter Two
Rupert Goes to School 8

Chapter Three
Marmalade on the Prowl! 18

Chapter Four
On the Roof 32

CHAPTER ONE
Scary Ladder

Martin's mum was at the top of a ladder, painting the house.

"It's an incredible view from up here," she said.

"Let me see," said Martin.

Martin's mum came down. She held the ladder while Martin climbed up. The ladder moved slightly as Martin climbed higher.

Halfway up, Martin looked down.
The ground was a long way off.
Everything looked smaller.

Martin felt giddy.

He was scared.

He didn't want to go any higher.

He came down,

gripping the ladder tightly.

Martin went inside
to look at Rupert, his pet rat.
Rupert was more fun
than climbing a ladder.
He lived in a cage
that Martin's dad had made.

Rupert had white fur,
a pink nose, and a long tail.
His whiskers twitched
when Martin gave him food.

The next day, Martin told his teacher all about his pet rat.

"Why don't you bring Rupert to school?" said Miss Clark. "We're studying rodents. We can write about him."

CHAPTER TWO
Rupert Goes to School

A couple of days after Martin tried to climb the ladder, he took Rupert to school.

The children all liked Rupert.
They watched him eat
bits of cheese, apple, and bread.
When he squeaked,
the children all squeaked.
When he sat up and sniffed,
everyone sat up and sniffed.
Then they wanted to hold Rupert.

Martin took Rupert out of his cage. He held Rupert carefully as everyone touched his fur.

"No loud noises, children," said Miss Clark.

Andrea rushed over to see Rupert.
She banged into Martin's desk.
Sometimes Andrea was
a little clumsy.

Rupert was frightened. He jumped out of Martin's hands and ran along the floor.

The children tried to catch Rupert, but that only scared him more.

"Stay back, children!" said Miss Clark. "Let Martin catch poor Rupert."

Martin saw Rupert hiding under a cupboard. Rupert was trembling.

Martin walked towards him.
"Easy, Rupert," he said. "Easy."
Just as Martin went to grab
Rupert, Andrea bent down to have
a look. She knocked over a chair.

Rupert jumped, ran across the room until he came to the open door, and dashed outside.

"Oh no!" said the children.

"Oh no!" said Miss Clark.

"Oh *no*!" said Martin.

The children ran outside to look for Rupert. He had disappeared, completely disappeared.

CHAPTER THREE
Marmalade on the Prowl!

Martin was very worried.
Rupert had trusted him,
but Martin had taken Rupert
out of his safe home.
Now Rupert was lost, and Martin
might never see him again.

Everyone hunted for Rupert.

They looked under buildings.

They looked under bushes.

But they didn't see Rupert.

Then Mr Loretto, the caretaker, ran up.

"A white rat just shot up the drainpipe on the shed. It must be on the roof somewhere. I'll call Marmalade. She'll fix it!"

Martin was shocked. He had forgotten all about the school cat.

Marmalade would catch Rupert and kill him!

Martin turned to Mr Loretto.

"Don't call Marmalade. That rat is Rupert! He's my pet!"

It was too late.

Marmalade was already sniffing around the drainpipe.

Then she looked up and meowed.

Marmalade wanted to climb onto the roof and hunt Rupert.

Mr Loretto went into the shed. He came out with a ladder. He put it against the wall.

"Don't worry. I'll climb up and get Rupert before Marmalade does," said Mr Loretto.

Martin remembered the wobbly ladder he'd climbed. He was glad that Mr Loretto was climbing the ladder instead of him.

Marmalade didn't need a ladder. She was already climbing up a tree next to the shed, using her sharp claws.

Mr Loretto climbed to the top of the ladder. Then he got up onto the roof. It seemed high. It looked dangerous.

Mr Loretto walked around the roof, looking for Rupert.

The children heard him trying to scare off the cat.

"Hiss! Hiss! Go away, Marmalade!"

Then Mr Loretto called down to Martin.

"I've found Rupert!" he said. "The trouble is he won't come to me, and Marmalade is up here."

CHAPTER FOUR
On the Roof

Martin swallowed. Only he could save Rupert. He walked over to the ladder. He started to climb.

"Martin!" shouted Miss Clark. "It's too dangerous up there!"

Martin kept on climbing. He was determined to save his pet. Miss Clark held the ladder steady for Martin.

"Please, be careful, Martin," she said, with a worried voice. Martin was afraid, but he climbed all the way to the top.

Then Mr Loretto helped Martin climb onto the roof.

"Good climbing," he said.

Martin tried not to look down.

"Where's Rupert?" he asked.

Mr Loretto pointed to the gutter. Martin crept over, still holding Mr Loretto's hand. The roof creaked.

Martin was high above the playground. He could see a long way down the street. He could also see Rupert hiding at the end of the gutter.

Rupert was shivering.
His whiskers drooped.
He was wet from some water
that was in the gutter.

"Easy, Rupert," said Martin. Martin carefully and slowly moved his hands forward. Martin caught Rupert.

Martin realized that he would have to put Rupert in his cage before climbing down the ladder.

"I need the cage, please," he said to Mr Loretto.

"The cage!" Mr Loretto shouted down to Miss Clark.

"Get the cage, please," Miss Clark said to Andrea.

Andrea rushed into the classroom and got the cage. This time, she didn't knock into anything.

41

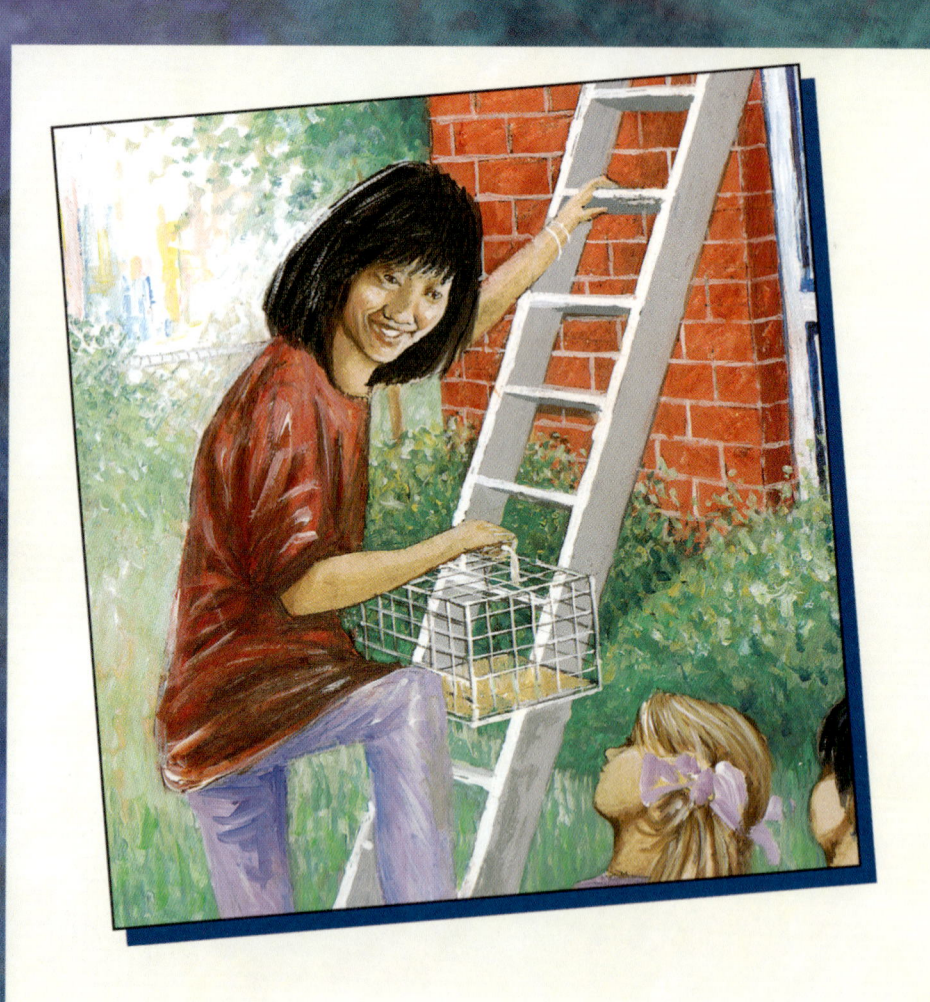

Miss Clark took the cage from Andrea and slowly climbed up the ladder with the cage in one hand.

When she reached the top, Miss Clark opened the door of the cage. Carefully, Martin put Rupert inside. Then Miss Clark closed the door.

At last, Rupert was safe.

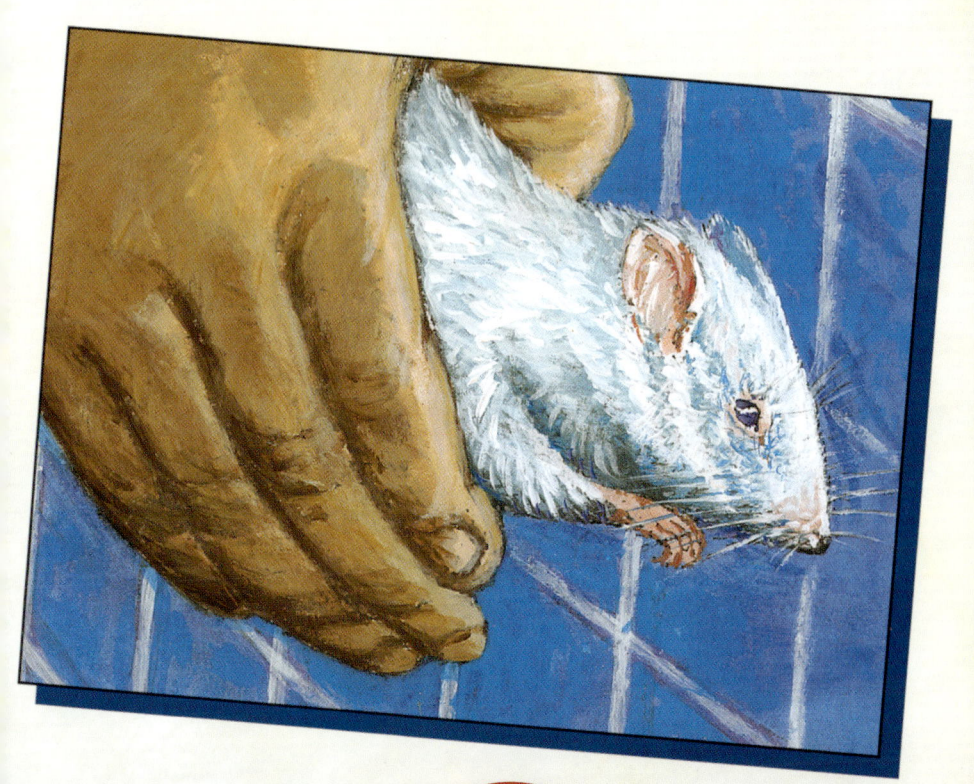

The children clapped and cheered. Martin felt scared and tired and happy, all at the same time.

Miss Clark smiled at Martin.

"Excellent job, Martin," she said. "You were very brave."

45

Martin looked at the trees and the sky. He smiled, too.

"You know, it's an incredible view from up here!" he said.

From the Author

One weekend, I was painting the house, and my daughter brought home a pet rat to take care of. That's how I got the idea for writing this story.

John Parker

From the Illustrator

I live near the beach with my wife, son, and daughter. We have two dogs and a large pond with twenty-six fish! I really like stories about pets.

Mark Wilson

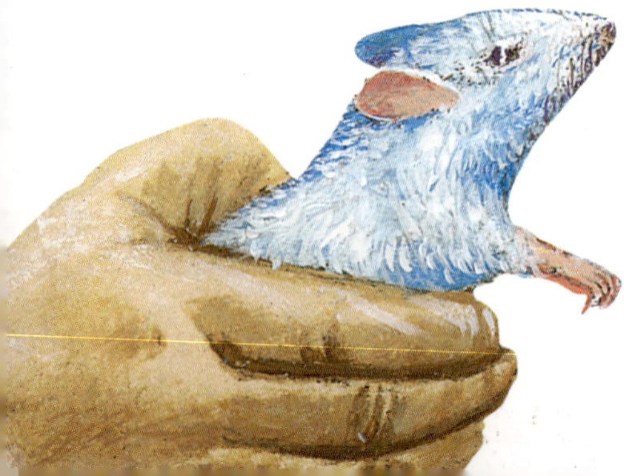